Landon, the Superhero of the Worlds!

Landon, the Superhero of the Worlds!

Titus Andrew M. Bonifacio

Rev. date: 04/24/2014

**To order additional copies of this book,
log on to:**
www.titusbonifacio.com
or contact:
Xlibris LLC
1-888-795-4274
www.Xlibris.com
Orders@Xlibris.com
552216

ACKNOWLEDGEMENTS

I want to thank all the genious people who invented ink, computers, paper, and the company who made my first book possible. This book would not exist without them. Also, I want to thank my friends, teachers, and most importantly, my family; especially my Mom who has always believed that I could do this and for asking me to publish this story. Thank you, Mom, for guiding me all through the process of this book. I love you, Mom, very much.

One day, in New York City, a boy named Landon was walking home from school. While walking home, he noticed a neighbor's house on fire. He quickly dashed to the house and tried to put out the fire. He put out half of the fire. He went inside the house, trying to save a crying old man. Then, something strange happened. The fire grew bigger and bigger, and then another fire appeared with different colors, like a rainbow, floating on the air, moving toward him. He was so surprised and couldn't believe what he saw. There was a quick blast of lightning that entered his body.

"Wow!" said Landon.

He tried to run but couldn't move his feet. He shouted for help, but nobody heard him. The rainbow fire began circling around Landon and also entered inside his body and transformed him into something different.

"Super Landon!" said the rainbow fire.

He magically became a "super" kid, stronger, faster, and had tremendous energy. It appeared that he was given superpowers. His superpowers were superspeed, fire-shooting hands, flying, and an icy breath.

"Wow! What happened to me? What is going on?" questioned Landon, surprised.

He felt so strong, brave, and unstoppable.

"Now, I can save the man!" exclaimed Landon.

He ran fast, trying to find the old man.

"Help! Help! Help me!" screamed the crying old man.

Landon blew an icy wind around the old man. The ice melted, quickly turning into water that put the fire out. The man's skin color was red, and the water had soaked him to the bone. His hair, his face, and everything else were wet. The man turned slowly and smiled beautifully at Landon, saying, "Thank you for saving me."

Landon didn't notice that there were firemen and a crowd of people outside that saw everything he did for the old man.

"Yeyhey! You are a superkid! Superkid!" cheered the people and the firemen, applauding.

"Who is this kid?" asked the other fireman, looking happily at Landon.

After all the people left, a superhero was now born in one of the busiest boroughs in New York City. His name was Super Landon! But like in all superheroes' lives, there was always a supervillain and he was just around the corner. His name was Pistacio. He was the supervillain of dark lightning, waiting for years to find a superhero to destroy him as Pistacio wanted to rule the world. Before he could do that, he would have to destroy Cat World because he hated cats!

Meanwhile, down at Earth inside Landon's room, Landon was trying out his new powers . . . .

"These superpowers are great! I can do chores faster!" said Landon happily.

"Landon!" his mom called him from the kitchen.

"Yes, Mom?" answered Landon.

"Time for lunch," said his mom.

Landon rushed quickly downstairs to get lunch and rushed back to his room like a bolt of lightning, his feet not even touching the stairs, his body flying through the air as though he were a falcon diving to the ground, looking for food.

"Now it's time to watch my favorite TV show, *Teen Titan Rockets Go!*" said Landon excitedly.

While watching TV inside his room, Landon got a strange call from the power plant.

"Hello! Hello! Anyone, help! The power plant is being destroyed by some sort of power! If you're getting this message, you need to call 955!" said the strange voice from the other line.

"Hello! Hello! Are you still there?" asked Landon.

Beep!

The call ended right away, and Landon put the phone down curiously. He turned off the TV and flew to his friend's house.

"Brandon! Brandon!" yelled Landon, knocking the door and looking for his friend outside the house.

"What? I'm busy right now!" Brandon said.

"No, you're not! You're just playing video games!" replied Landon, excited. Brandon paused his game and walked toward the door and opened it.

"Why are you here? It's not time for our game yet," Brandon asked.

"I just got a weird call from the power plant, and they gave me a number to call but not the whole phone number," said Landon.

"What power plant? That sounds big! Well, let's start looking and working! We can try every number we can think of to find the caller," said Brandon.

"Okay, let's start now!" said Landon.

The friends worked for an hour until they found the man named the Catman. The number was from another planet, called Cat World.

"I can't believe the cat is on a different planet!" said Landon, shocked.

"Me too!" answered Brandon.

"How are we supposed to get to another planet?" anxiously asked Landon.

"No way! That's millions of miles away from my house! That's impossible! What are we going to do?" asked Brandon.

"I know that!" Landon said.

Landon needed to think about what to do next, and suddenly it occurred to him . . .

"No, you can't get there, but I can!" exclaimed Landon.

"What do you mean, Landon?" asked his confused best friend again.

"Remember the fire incident the other day?" said Landon.

"Yeah—yeah . . ." answered Brandon while nodding his head and his eyes grew bigger and bigger.

"When I tried to help the old man, there was a blast of lightning, and magical fire circling around me and it transformed me into a superhero. I never told anyone about it, not even my mom," explained Landon.

"Really? You are kidding, right?"

"Why? I mean, how did it happen? Who gave it to you, and why you? I'm more . . . than you?" jealously asked Brandon.

"Okay, you're my best friend, I'm okay with that, so you meant to say you only told me this now?" asked Brandon.

"Yes, and I'm not kidding. I am serious! So please don't be jealous of me. I'm sorry I'm the only one who can go to Cat World" kindly said Landon.

"So I guess I won't see you for a little while," said Brandon.

"I guess this is good-bye then?" asked Landon.

"Yeah, I guess," Brandon answered sadly.

They both said their good-byes. Landon hugged his best friend tightly, and then he went off to Cat World. He flew very fast into outer space, but when he got there, Landon was too late.

By the time he landed at Cat World, everything was gone. All he saw were cats' footprints on the ground, and there was only one cat that survived, one of their police officers.

"What happened here?" Landon asked the wounded cat police officer."

"Pistacio, the dark lightning and supervillainous man, like you, came down here with everything he had and destroyed our planet," the cat police officer explained.

"Are there any other people, I mean, like you here that are still alive?" asked Landon.

"I don't know," answered the police officer.

"What did Pistacio look like?" Landon asked.

"He has a mustache, hairy eyebrows, and static hair, and the hairiest eyebrows that I have ever seen," said the police officer, referring to the eyebrows again.

"I guess that leads me to my next question. Do you know where he is going to strike next?" asked Landon.

"A planet named Earth. I heard him commanding his army to find a superhero there, to destroy him, and to rule the entire world," said the police officer.

"Well, Earth is my planet, so I'm going back where I came from!" said Landon bravely.

"You can't live here anymore. All I can see is the bright catlight, I mean your sunlight, and that . . ." He pointed at the catsy dark waterfalls. "Unless you want to come with me to our world," said Landon.

"Yes! I want to come with you and leave this place. What can I do here now?" asked the cat police officer.

"You better hold on tight because we're going for a road trip," said Landon.

Whooooosh! Ohhhh! Yeeesss!

The two took off and enjoyed the Cat World's wind rushing into their faces, cat's fur blowing everywhere, and then they vanished. In a total of fifty seconds, they landed in New York City.

"Does this thing have any brakes?" the police officer asked, nervously pointing out Landon's cape.

"No, it doesn't," Landon said, and he pulled the police officer from his back and put him down.

"You never told me your name," said Landon.

"Furry, my name is Furry," said the police officer. The officer saluted, and took Landon's right hand and shook it vigorously while thanking Landon for the ride.

"Oh, my name is Landon."

"Nice to meet you, Landon. Thank you for bringing me here to your world and saving me from the Cat World," said the police officer.

"You're welcome, Officer!"

"Well, we're here, and it looks like Pistacio didn't arrive yet, so that means we still have time to meet Brandon, my best friend," said Landon.

"Okay, I would love to meet him," said Furry.

Landon was about to ring the doorbell as Brandon was trying to leave their house. He walked toward the door and rang the doorbell.

Ding! Dong!

Brandon opened the door and exclaimed, "Landon, you're back and you brought a friend who's dressed up as a cat pol—"

"This is Furry. He is a police officer from Cat World."

"Hi! Nice to meet you, Furrrr!" said Brandon.

"Thank you! Nice to meet you, Brarrr!" said Furry while trying to salute Brandon.

"When I arrived there, Furry was the only cat, I mean, person, I found. I'm not sure if there were others left behind, or maybe they were hiding because they're scared."

"That's right, maybe, but we don't have to worry about that now because we need to find Furry a place to sleep for a couple of days," explained Landon.

"Yes! Maybe he can stay with you down in the basement because cats still need to eat, right?" asked Brandon.

"Yes, of course!"

"It's just maybe I thought you could share your room and your food with Furry," answered Landon.

"I don't know about that because you know, Kendall can be a little feisty when it comes to food," said Brandon.

"Oh yeah! While I fix things for a little while with Pistacio and I am saving the world, would you please do this little favor for me? Plus I don't even have a pet, so it would be weird if my mom saw me with cat food inside the house," explained Landon again.

"Fine. I'll do it, but on one condition," said Brandon.

"What is it, my friend?" asked Landon.

"You have to come to the talent show next month," said Brandon.

"Why? Is it really important to you that I come?" asked Landon.

"Yes, you didn't come when we were in first grade, third grade, or fourth grade! I want you to come with me this year!" requested Brandon.

The two agreed, so Brandon told Furry all the house rules, and Landon tried to think, why would Pistacio come to Earth, and what would be his next move?

Landon decided to go home because his mom would probably wonder where he was. He flew back to his house and went to his bedroom's window with lightning speed and tried to be normal as he should be, sitting on his chair in front of his study table.

"Landon, this is my second call. Where are you?" his mom said.

"I'll be right there, Mom. Just need to finish a project," said Landon. When Landon left to see his mom, his project came to life.

Rumble! Rumble! Sssssssssss!

"So, Landon, how was your day?" asked his mom while reading her magazine, sitting on her favorite red couch.

"Great, Mom! Thank you for asking."

"How about yours?" asked Landon, playing his Puzzle Cube.

While Landon was talking, his mom noticed something moving toward her, and his mom saw Landon's superpowers for the first time.

"Must destroy everything! Must destroy everything!" the nightmare robot said.

"Aahh!" both Landon and his mom shrieked.

"Target sighted!" said the robot, pointing at his mom.

"Destroy target! Destroy target!" said the robot.

"Helppp! Landon! Landon, run!" shouted his mom, horribly scared.

The robot was ready to fire his laser beams at her. Landon then used his ice-wind breath to freeze him and threw one fireball on the robot's body to melt it.

"Landon, be careful—watch out! Come here!" Mom shouted at him while covering her body on the back of the couch. His mom saw Landon transformed into Super Landon for the first time.

"Wow! Landon, you saved my life. Oh! No! You're not Landon! You're not my son!" his mom screamed, scared and confused.

"Mom! Mom! Calm down, it's me, your son, Landon! See!" Landon showed his right thumb like a thumbs-up, his thumb bent almost touching the skin and looking like a letter C.

"My son!" cried his mother. "Landon! My son! Are you okay?" His mother was so worried and horrified at what she saw. "Thank you, my son! You saved my life!" said his mom while hugging and kissing Landon on his head.

"You're welcome, Mom!"

"Where did those robots come from?"

"I don't know, Mom. They look like my drawing project!"

"But how did you get all the powers and that cape? Where did they come from? Answer me!" demanded his mom, shocked.

"Remember when I told you I saved that old man?"

"Yes," answered his mom, confused.

"Well," stuttered Landon, "this amazing fire circled around me and gave me these superpowers."

"Who? How? Why? Why didn't you tell me about this?" asked his mom again, stunned.

"Because I thought you would get mad at me and keep me inside the house," said Landon, sheepishly.

"Oh, honey!" his mom said sympathetically, putting her arms around him. "I would never get mad if you're being honest with me, unless you used your superpowers for something bad."

"I'm very sorry, Mom. I'm sorry for not telling you about my superpowers, and don't worry, Mom, I think we're safe now," said Landon, assuring his mom.

"That's all I needed to hear," said his mom calmly.

So Landon and his mom agreed to not tell anyone about the superpowers. Landon told his mom about the trip in outer space and about Furry staying in Brandon's house.

Three hours later, in Pistacio's galaxy . . .

"Well, the superhero might have destroyed my robot destroyers, but he doesn't know what's coming next after him. Mwah! Ha! Ha! Ha! Ha! Ha!" Pistacio laughed evilly.

"Oh, poor Landon he doesn't know that I sent those robots to spy on him," said Pistacio.

"Pistacio, your ninja destroyers are here," said one of his minions.

"Ah, yes! My ninja destroyers, the best destroyers in the galaxy!"

"Yes, we are the finest and best ones, of course!" said the ninja destroyer captain.

"Great! There's a superhero that needs to be taught a lesson."

"Which superhero shall we destroy, Master Pistacio?" asked the captain.

"Landon, the superhero!"

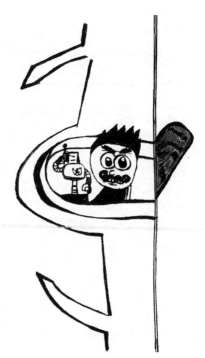

"We shall destroy him for you!" said the robots, shouting and cheering for their master.

Now, Superhero Landon was in danger. The big battle was soon to come. How would Landon protect himself if he is supposed to protect others? What should Landon, the Superhero, do? Pistacio had everything he needed to put Landon down.

At Brandon's house, the phone rang.

"Hello, Brandon? It's me, your friend." "I got all the spare parts from a robot who tried to destroy my mom and I. According to my fire analysis, it turns out that the robots were sent to destroy us. Pistacio replaced our project robots with his."

"Wait! Wait a minute! I have two questions," asked Brandon. "First, why are you just telling me this now; that a robot destroyer almost destroyed you and your mom? Second, I didn't say you had to do all of the work yourself, because I remember Mr. Bernard said we both have to do the work for the project as a team.

I could help you with the project because we all know I have watched every robot movie on TV Land and I'm basically a robot maniac myself, which means I know all about robots," said Brandon.

"Oh yeah! Why did I forget that?" said Landon sarcastically. "I'm just kidding!" he replied afterward.

"You should have come to my house or talked to me at school or whenever you saw me. You know that I'm always busy!" said Landon.

"You could have come to my place because I have so many facts about robots, and I'm going to say what I said before," retorted Brandon. "I know everything about robots and I have *all* the facts!"

"Maybe I would've. If you weren't acting like my dad and nagging me right now, I wouldn't have to tell you to help me with the robot, and I could have just gone to your house now!" said Landon, getting tired of Brandon's attitude.

The two got into an argument for over an hour, afterwards, they apologized to each other, then, they decided to do their own projects and hung up the phone.

The next morning, Landon was walking home from school, and out of nowhere, a ninja robot destroyer army appeared and attacked Landon.

"Target sighted. Set blasters to stun," voiced the robot destroyers.

"Oh no, you don't!" shouted Landon.

Landon charged up his fireball. It grew bigger and bigger. He threw the fireball, and it went straight towards the ninja destroyers. Nothing happened as fireballs wouldn't work against ninjas. They could only be hit with shadows, so the fireballs went right past them.

"Oh no! I can't fight them with my powers, but I think I can just use my karate skills to defeat them," said Landon.

He ran fast with his new superspeed and found a shadow so he could fight now.

"You fool! You can't beat a ninja," said the captain of the ninja destroyers.

"Mr. Ninja, you are not nice! Don't say that, please! Oh, I forgot you're a robot, so maybe you will learn your lesson. Well, I can try!" exclaimed Landon.

They fought and fought . . . *Boom! Crush! Pow!*

They were both going head-on, but near the end, our hero and the ninja destroyers were getting very tired, but they still fought until the very end. At the end, there could only be the strongest left standing.

"Man, aren't you guys tired? I need to take a rest," said Landon.

"Ninja warriors don't rest!" said the ninja destroyer captain. "Fight now! Fight now!"

"Landon, the superhero, you shall be destroyed! Ha, ha, ha! What!?"

After four hours of fighting, the ninja destroyers might have been silent, but they weren't good at being invisible. Another hero, not a superhero, named Jaime, came to help the Superhero Landon from the ninja destroyers. "Take that! And that! You robots, here I come!" shouted Jaime.

"Wow! Nice moves!" said Landon before he fainted, exhausted from the heat.

He missed the end of the fight and didn't witness how Jaime finished it.

"Ahh, what happened here?" questioned Landon, still groggy from having passed out. "Did I faint after a girl beat all those bushy ninja destroyers?" questioned Landon weakly.

"Yes. You fainted from the heat, and that *girl* you mentioned was me, Jaime. I rescued you!" said Jaime.

"What? You rescued me from the ninja destroyers?" questioned Landon, confused. "How did you end the fight?"

"Because I was once like you, but Pistacio is the controller of dark lightning and the one who took my powers. If you don't defeat him, he'll take your superpowers away forever!" exclaimed Jaime.

"Pistacio didn't know that I saved one last thing for myself," said Jaime.

"Well, this Pistacio guy is bad and extremely dangerous to all of us, even to those minions. He's a bad influence to those robots, so could you help me deal with him, please?" asked Landon nicely.

"Okay, I will train you," said Jaime.

So our new superhero started training with the old superhero, Jaime, and things were going great!

However, unbeknownst to Jaime and Landon, Pistacio and the ninja warriors continued to plot their evil ways.

"Now that most of my ninja destroyers were destroyed, I have to go down to Earth to destroy this so-called superhero, Landon!" said Pistacio dangerously. "I will take over the entire world with my new companion! HA! HA! HA!"

Suddenly, Brandon appeared from a dark corner and was now inside Pistacio's galaxy! Pistacio and Brandon began preparing all the destroyers for the invasion. What was Landon going to do? Our hero wasn't supposed to fight Pistacio along with his best friend, Brandon, by himself, but most importantly, he didn't have an army.

That morning, inside Landon's backyard, Landon and Jaime were just getting up for the day.

"Ahhh." Landon stretched. "What a great morning! Let's train!" he said excitedly to Jaime.

At the same time, Pistacio and Brandon were getting ready as well . . .

"Charge! Ready the destroyers, Brandon!" said Pistacio.

"Yes, master!" said Brandon as he prepared to launch the attack against New York City.

Then inside New York City, the unexpected was happening . . .

"Ahh! Ahh! It's the aliens! Aliens are here!" screeched a young mother, trying to protect her young child.

"Ahh! Run for your life!" screamed a mailman.

People were panicking and terrified. They were running and bumping into one another; children were crying.

"Fire at those tall buildings!" Brandon ordered the destroyers.

Meanwhile, Landon and Jaime were still training in their backyard, at the park, at the gym, and even underneath the Brooklyn Bridge.

"Jaime! We need to be strong! Strong! Come on, let's keep training!" encouraged Landon bravely while kicking and punching the air.

"Are you kidding? Pistacio's sidekick and the destroyers are destroying the city!" said Jaime, panicking.

"Okay, Jaime!"

"I suppose you have a plan," asked Landon while still kicking and punching.

"I thought you had a plan!" answered Jaime. Suddenly, Jaime realized something bad was happening. "Oh no! We are screwed. We have to run! They're here!" shouted Jaime.

"No! We have to fight back so we can win back our city!" said Landon bravely again.

"Okay then, I need you to fly me up there." Jaime pointed up. "And then drop me down to the ship while you take care of the destroyers," she said.

"I hope your plan works, because if it doesn't, there will be no more New York City!" exclaimed Landon.

"I hope so too," said Jaime.

"Okay, let's go! Wait, I can't go now," said Landon.

"Why?" asked Jaime.

"I forgot my belt," said Landon.

"Landon, you don't need your belt, you're a superhero, and superheroes don't need regular belts, believe me!" said Jaime.

So now Jaime and our superhero Landon were going to fight back, but what about the army of Pistacio's destroyers? Landon didn't even have any help besides Jaime. How could they possibly defeat Pistacio's army?

"Okay, Landon, here we go," Pistacio mumbled to himself, plotting for his victory while inspecting his army and busy preparing for their biggest battle.

Landon and Jaime were aiming to reach Pistacio's ship to get closer to Pistacio's launchpad.

"Wow! That thing is huge!" said Jaime.

"Yeah, it is! Don't worry, size doesn't matter. It's the effort you put in that matters." answered Landon.

"What?" asked Jaime.

"I can't hear you!" said Landon to Jaime, and ran away from her.

"Landon, whatever happens, don't go near Pistacio yet!" advised Jaime to Landon. She herself was planning to make of a great move and preparing herself.

"Okay!" said Landon.

Meanwhile, inside Pistacio's shiny and very clean ship, Jaime had reached the base of the battle station. Landon had to find out how to stop the ship and Pistacio's wicked plans and the destroyers.

"Landon, how are you doing down there?" asked Jaime.

"Good! I'm glad you asked because I need to warn you to brace for impact," answered Landon.

"What! Why?" asked Jaime.

"I'm preparing something here to hit the side of Pistacio's ship, just to scare Pistacio. He is really close!" warned Landon.

"What? No!" shouted Jaime back to Landon.

"It's too late! Now, embrace for impact, in five . . . four . . . three . . . two . . . one." *Boom!!!*

"Jaime, do you read?" asked Landon while touching his headset .

"Yeah! Please promise me, do not do that again," requested Jaime.

"Okay, I'm just testing the whole impact thing," said Landon.

The phone rang from Landon's headset .

Ring! Ring! Ring!

Landon pressed his headset and answered the call.

"Hello!" said Landon.

"Landon! You're all over the news! There's something I need to tell you about Brandon," said Landon's mom on the phone.

"Mom, is that you? What?" asked Landon, surprised.

"Brandon has sided with Pistacio," said his mom.

"No! It can't be. How did that happen? He would never do that!" said Landon.

Landon's mom paused for a moment and said worriedly, "I just thought that you should know that."

When Landon was done talking to his mom, he looked sad and confused.

On the other side of the ship, inside Pistacio's battle station, Pistacio looked at the window and saw Landon's red cape flowing and flying around Landon's body.

"There he is! Fire!" commanded Pistacio to his army. Instead of stunning Landon, the shot hit a hospital and destroyed it. Pistacio used a laser to shoot and set some buildings on fire. This was the time that Pistacio realized that he was really bad because he could see all the people screaming, crying, and running from everywhere.

"Brandon, get Landon and bring him here so we can have a discussion!" commanded Pistacio.

"Yes, master!" answered Brandon while saluting Pistacio.

Then later on, Pistacio gave some more orders to Brandon.

"Brandon, stop shootings! I want Landon to surrender! Page his name. Use the loudspeaker so everybody can hear it. He is your friend, he will listen to you.

Ask him to get to the lower base, to the war zone. If he really wants to end this war, ask him to surrender himself. We can settle our agreements there," demanded Pistacio again.

Brandon followed Pistacio's order and tried to find Landon. They didn't realize that Landon could sense them and he heard their conversation.

"Brandon, where are you going? If you want me to surrender, you better stop this war first!" said Landon.

Landon landed in front of his best friend. He came from nowhere like a thunderclap and was now standing bravely, facing toward his best friend. Brandon was so surprised and didn't know what to do.

Brandon ran quickly heading to Pistacio's location.

Landon also ran and went inside the base. He saw Pistacio and Brandon discussing their aggressive plan.

Landon was shocked to realize how bad his best friend was now. He couldn't believe the truth: that his best friend, Brandon, turned into another Pistacio, an overlord, was really true.

"Well, hello there, my old friend!" said Brandon.

Landon was confused and answered his bestfriend. "Hello, Brandon. How can you do this to me and to your family? You, you're my best friend!" said Landon.

"Well, not anymore, Landon! Pistacio told me that if I help him track you down, my family and I will not be enslaved by him, and both of us can rule the world. Nobody can stop us now!" said Brandon.

"Except me!" answered Landon.

Pistacio heard Landon's answer. He was so mad. His mustache looked so messy, and the hairs were crisscrossing each other.

"I don't think so, because the contract you are about to sign states that you will surrender your powers, and if you don't sign it, all of New York City will be gone and you will be enslaved by our army," said Brandon.

Pistacio suddenly appeared in front of Landon and looked directly into his eyes.

"What Brandon was trying to say is *my* army will come to hunt you if you don't sign the contract!" said Pistacio.

Landon stopped for a moment to think, walking away, and then turned to say, "Before I will sign the contract, I want to know why you became so bad and hated almost everything." looking deeply into Pistacio's eyes.

After asking a question, Landon came back forward and looked at Pistacio's eyes again.

"I did a search about you. When you were a little kid, you were bullied almost every week. You didn't tell your parents because you wanted to go to school every day. Year after year, you learned to fight back. Sometimes you ended up in a fight or turned tables over at school to get everybody's attention and threw things around. For a while, you were a problem, even for your parents," said Landon.

Pistacio just stood there, unmoving. Brandon tried to speak but couldn't. Nothing came out of his mouth.

Landon was still talking. "Later on, you bullied almost all the kids, especially those who bullied you before. Then later, you ran away from your parents, and that was the start. You changed and became so bad and never came back to your family. Your parents tried very hard to find you."

Pistacio continued to listen to his flashback story.

"There's nothing to be afraid of anymore, Pistacio," said Landon.

Suddenly, Pistacio moved and yelled, "I don't believe you. You're my enemy!"

"You're a big boy now. Your parents need you, Pistacio," said Landon again.

Pistacio was so angry, and he blushed. "I'm the greatest and the strongest, I don't need to listen to you!"

"I thought you needed somebody, somebody who truly cares about you! Your parents, your family, Pistacio! You need to see them again. They miss you so much, and I know you too as well."

Pistacio pushed Landon away from him, but Landon didn't stop and still tried to convince Pistacio. He was trying to be friendly and nice. "I found your parents and brought them here so you would know that they really care about you."

Landon moved and turned slowly around. His cape was also turning, flying and blowing majestically in the air, and dropped slowly as if in slow motion on the ground, when he jumped over to the other side of the ship. He pointed out to Pistacio's parents at the other corner.

"Mr. and Mrs . . . come on in!" said Landon.

Pistacio's parents walked out from the dark corner and were so excited to see their son. "Pistacio!"

"No! No! Don't move!" shouted Pistacio while running towards his parents.

While Pistacio's parents were running, eagerly and excitedly, to see their son. They both tripped over something probably a wire hidden on the ground. Then the wire created a heavy smoke and there was something else that came out and splashed all over like red laser beams in the air that looked like red lava scattered in space. Pistacio's parents were horrified and laid down on the ground quickly.

Landon saw everything and was totally surprised, and again he flew like thunder in the air and grabbed all the red laser beams and wrapped them with his cape.

"Pistacio! Run and get your parents away from here!" said Landon, then he flew toward the window and went off away from them.

"Mom! Dad! Come over here!" said Pistacio, scared, and ran over to his parents.

Pistacio's parents tried to get up and grabbed Pistacio's hand.

"Oh, Pistacio, what have you done? It has been so long since we saw you. What happened to you?" asked Pistacio's dad.

Pistacio knelt down over to his parents' feet then got up and hugged his mother and his father, crying like a baby.

"So as your father, I am so concerned about you. We never thought you would turn out this way. Your mother and I urge you to stop being a supervillain."

Pistacio's mother was still hugging Pistacio, and eventually she said something. "We need you and we want you to grow up, go to college, and live a happy life. Please stay at home with us so we can see you every day."

"We are your family. We love you," said Pistacio's father.

Pistacio's mother pulled something out from her purse and showed it off to Pistacio. "Do you know this picture, remember this?" his mother asked him.

"No," replied Pistacio.

"This is you when you were a baby. Come home with us, and I will show you more, you don't need to worry about anything anymore," said his mother, calmed and relaxed.

Pistacio hugged his mother and his father. "Okay, Mom and Dad."

The three reunited and looked very happy.

Meanwhile, Jaime was running hurriedly and was worried, looking for Landon. "Landon! Landon!"

Landon just flew back from outside the ship. "Yes, Jaime, I'm here."

"We have to go now! This thing is going to explode!" said Jaime.

"Explode? What do you mean, explode!" exclaimed Landon.

"I put lots of soda volcanoes next to the engine room to create some explosions!" answered Jaime.

"Can you stop it?" Landon asked.

"No, it's exploding right—"

Boom!

Jaime tried to run away and shouted, "Now!"

"I'll be right there by the launchpad," shouted Landon back to Jaime.

"Okay!" said Jaime, and went back.

"Everyone, we have to move now!" ordered Landon.

The explosions got Pistacio's attention.

"What happened? Why did the engine room explode?" Pistacio asked.

"My friend Jaime and I caused it. We did something," Landon replied.

"What did you do?" asked Pistacio again.

"We had this plan to stop you from ruling the world. What you heard was just our first simple idea that we created, and was supposed to scare you and your army to go away. I think we don't need to do our second or third nor fourth, right?" asked Landon.

Pistacio replied, "But that doesn't give you the right to attack my brand new ship!"

"Yes, it does," Landon answered.

Pistacio's mother stepped up and said, "Pistacio, Landon just saved our lives. Stop it. We need to go now. I think this ship will be . . ."

Pistacio's mother paused for a moment and looked into her son's eyes.

"You're right, Mom. I'm sorry. I thought about my army, they're in the engine room."

Pistacio apologized, and after that, he shut off his powered electric army using a hidden watch on his arm.

"I'm sorry too for putting soda volcanoes in your ship," Landon said.

Pistacio's arm was held by his father, then he said, "Since you two are now friends, let's think about how to get out of here."

"Do you know where the emergency exit is, Pistacio?" asked Landon.

"It's below the engine room, and we need to jump because it's the only way we can get out of here."

"Well, not for me, because I can fly and stop anytime I want to," said Landon.

"Wait, Landon, do you have superstrength?" asked Pistacio.

"Yes, of course! Why?"

Pistacio gathered everybody and asked Landon to carry them.

"Wait! No,no,no!" Landon retorted.

"Please, it's the only way to get down safely," said Pistacio.

"Fine, but this might hurt me," replied Landon.

Landon, the superhero, was carrying Pistacio and his parents outside the ship for a good reason: to get them down safely.

After taking care of Pistacio and his parents, Landon again had another problem. He forgot somebody. He had just lost Jaime.

"Where are you, Jaime! I can't find you!"

Landon kept looking, shouting Jaime's name and frantically worried.

"I'm near the platform!" shouted Jaime.

"Wait! I see you!" Landon shouted back.

"I see you too! I'm coming down. I'm carrying Pistacio and his parents." "Do you want to come too?" asked Landon.

"I can't fly. Yes, I do want to come!" Jaime shrieked.

Landon had to carry everybody out of Pistacio's warship safely.

"Okay, I can't carry anymore. So if you ask anyone else if I can carry them, no! No! I can't! Everyone, get ready. It's gonna be a bumpy ride!" said Landon.

"Aнннн! Aнннн! Yoooo ноооо!" shouted Landon gleefully.

Jaime screamed, "Landon, watch out!"

Landon replied, "Thanks, Jaime. Boy, that was a fun ride, wasn't it?"

Jaime shouted back, "No, it wasn't! We almost got crushed!"

"Okay then, but now we have to—" said Pistacio.

Pistacio was interrupted by a woman screaming below.

"Help! Help! Anyone help!" screamed the woman inside her car.

All of them saw her too, and they started to get scared.

Landon shouted back, "I'll be right there, ma'am."

The woman was frantically screaming, "Help! My baby and I are stuck! The train is heading towards us!"

Landon shouted back, "Okay, ma'am, just hang on, I'll be right there!"

Landon put everybody down and ran so fast to the car. While he was trying to use his powers, he noticed something very different this time.

He wasn't so fast at all like he was a couple of hours ago. He tried all his powers; he used the fireball and the icy breath. He even tried to fly, but he couldn't fly anymore. His body just fell down on the ground. He ran fast again but just got his normal speed. Everything went back to normal so quickly.

The train was almost there. Everybody just looked at Landon. They didn't know what was going on and that Landon was now a normal kid.

Even though Landon's powers were gone, he didn't give up. He pushed himself and tried very hard.

He saw a big stone and picked it up from the ground. He used the stone and all his strength to break the glass window. He was focused and prayed that he could still do something. He believed he could do it and still save the woman and the baby inside the car.

After Landon did a lot of pushing and bumping and trying his best to pry the car door while using the big stone just to get it open, the glass window finally cracked, and he opened the door.

Errrrrrrahhhhh!

Landon shouted to everybody, "Somebody needs to call 911!"

"What 911? You are the 911! We don't need them!" replied Pistacio.

Five seconds after Landon pulled the woman and her baby away from the car, the train just passed right by them.

Two minutes later, the fire truck and the ambulance came to the rescue.

The woman cried and carried her baby. "Thank you for saving us, Mr.?"

"Landon is my name, ma'am, and you're welcome. You and your baby are safe now," replied Landon.

Landon gave them a hug then turned to Pistacio.

"Pistacio, do you realize what you did here? That train was not supposed to be here, but because of your army, they messed up the train's control system."

Pistacio woefully replied, "Yes, and I promise to take full responsibility for the destruction I caused."

Landon said forcefully, "Okay, but you have to promise us to stop thinking of ruling the world again!"

His mom stepped up. "If you promise, everything will be great, then all of us will be together again."

Pistacio hugged his mom, and after that, he turned around and gratefully said, "Thank you, Super Landon, for teaching me to listen to my parents. They always know what's right. I realized everything now, how hard it is to be away from our family especially when you become bad as I was, everybody hates you. I don't want to do that again."

Landon looked so tired and just smiled.

"Thank you also for reminding me that bullying someone is a bad thing and always wrong. It can cause a lot of damage in our lives, and most of all, thank you for saving my parents' lives," Pistacio said sincerely.

"You're welcome, and please stay out of trouble now!"

Pistacio smiled back and said happily to Landon, "Yes, sir! I will!"

Then Pistacio saluted Landon.

Both laughed out loud, and everybody cheered.

Pistacio decided to end his evil ways and to be a good boy and forget about ruling the world for now. As a return favor, he promised Landon to help clean all the mess and to do his best to restore everything to normal again.

Landon's Superpowers

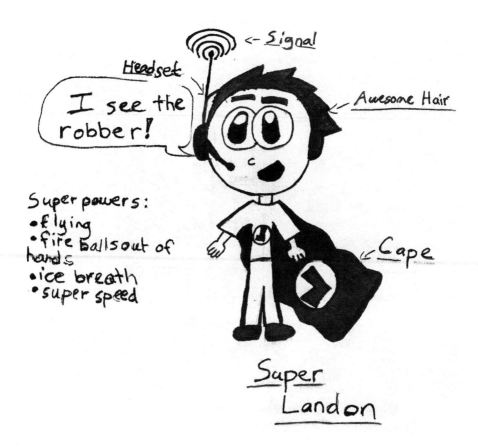

Landon's Family

Soon to be Our
Dog
(Fluffy)

Me

Mom

Dad

Our Family

**What do you think will happen to
Landon and Pistacio?**

What do you think will happen next?

Your Notes

Extra Page for you to Draw

Extra Page for you to Draw

Make Your Own Book Cover

You can add Jaime here if you want to or anything else. Use your imagination and be creative.

You may use your favorite colors.

Author's "Bonus" Drawing to the Reader

Titus Andrew M. Bonifacio is ten year old and is currently in 5th grade at St. Michael's school. He is passionate about drawing and writing stories from his own creative artwork. He also has cleverly created many types of artwork out of paper. He loves to play soccer, football, and tennis with his family. He plays on his school's flag football team. During the summer time, he also loves to go to the beach, swim at the pool, spend time with his family and friends, and exploring at Lego Land. Some of his favorite things to do during breaks at school is spending time with his friends. When he's not attending school, aside from writing and drawing, he loves to watch movies with his family, play video games, help his mom cooking or baking in the kitchen, but most of all go to the book store and ice cream parlor. When he was in kindergarten, he appeared on a local T.V. station and newspaper for winning 2nd place on a "Poster Drawing with Theme" contest. The winner was picked from students ranging from kindergarten to 5th grade and had participants from different schools. He won twice for the "Grandparents Day Creativity contest."

Thank you for buying this book and

hopefully for future books to come!

With detailed and expressive sketched illustrations, Titus Andrew M. Bonifacio has written an exciting adventure featuring a superhero who models bravery, respect, providing a help hand to others, and standing up to bullies. Quite a success for our young Author/Illustrator!

—Christine Evans, M.Ed., School Librarian

25309457R00052